ROSIE'S MOUSE
BY GINA & MERCER MAYER

For Grandma Rosie
& Grandma Evelyn

ROSIE'S MOUSE
BY GINA & MERCER MAYER

A GOLDEN BOOK • NEW YORK

Western Publishing Company, Inc., Racine, Wisconsin 53404

Rosie lived alone in a pink house. Her house was very neat. Her yard was very neat. Rosie liked everything to be neat.

But sometimes—especially at night after Rosie had tidied things up—the house seemed just too quiet and too neat. Then Rosie would get lonely.

One very neat night, Rosie was in fact feeling lonely. She called her neighbor, but the phone was busy. She called her sister, but no one was home.

Rosie had already finished reading her book. There was nothing else to do, so she went to bed.

That night Rosie dreamed something was tickling her feet. She woke up with a start. There *was* something tickling her feet. She turned on the light and threw off the covers.

There was a little brown mouse! He wriggled his nose at Rosie, jumped off the bed, and ran away.

"Mercy!" said Rosie. "A mouse in my neat bed! Ugh!" She changed the sheets and snuggled back into bed.

In the morning Rosie went to the kitchen to make coffee. What a mess! There were crumbs everywhere! A package of cookies was torn apart. A brand-new loaf of bread was ruined. Rosie's usually neat kitchen was a wreck.

"Looks like that mouse had fun in here," said Rosie.
It took her forever to make the kitchen neat again.

Then Rosie went to brush her teeth. There, sitting on the bathroom sink tasting the toothpaste, was the mouse!

Rosie snatched the tube away from him.
The mouse ran under the bathtub.

Rosie got dressed for her appointment at the beauty shop. On her way out the door, she reached into her purse for her keys. Instead of keys, she felt something furry. Rosie screamed. She dropped her purse on the floor. Out ran the little mouse.

At the beauty shop, Rosie told her friends about the mouse. They thought the idea of a mouse in Rosie's neat house was very funny. They called him Rosie's mouse. Rosie didn't think it was funny at all.

That afternoon Rosie's neighbor Evelyn came
over for tea. Rosie used her lovely china tea set, the
one handed down to her from Great Aunt Mirabella.
Evelyn picked up the pretty little sugar bowl,
lifted off the top . . .

. . . and out popped the little brown mouse. Evelyn
screamed. Everything flew in the air. Of course,
Evelyn was too upset to finish her tea, so she
went home.

Rosie cleaned up the mess. She was so embarrassed!

Later Rosie decided to take a bath. When she turned on the light in the bathroom, she saw her new box of bath beads spilled all over the floor. Her nightgowns were falling out of their drawer.

"That mouse is driving me crazy!" Rosie said to herself. "What will I do?"

After her bath Rosie snuggled into her nice soft, neat
bed. After a while she dozed off. Then she began
dreaming that someone was snoring in her ear.

Rosie turned on the light. The little mouse was

curled up on her pillow, fast asleep. She could hear his little snore.

Rosie was angry. She hit the pillow near the mouse with her hand. The mouse bounced into the air. Then the startled creature ran under the covers.

Rosie yanked all the covers off her neat little bed,
wadded them up, mouse and all, and threw them out the
front door.

"If you like my covers so much," she yelled,
"then sleep on them in the yard!"

For the rest of the night, Rosie slept with no covers at all. She was wrapped only in her bathrobe. All her sheets were either crumb-covered or full of holes.

In the morning Rosie sorted out her sheets.
The ones that had holes in them went in the
rag bag. The ones that didn't have holes
went to the laundry.

But when Rosie picked up the box of soap,
soap flakes came spilling out the bottom.
The mouse had chewed a big hole in the box.

"One more mess in my neat house!" Rosie
grumbled.

After lunch Rosie sat down to work on the sweater she was knitting. But the mouse had tangled the yarn so badly that it took her the rest of the afternoon to neaten her knitting.

When she happened to look through an old family
album, Rosie saw that the mouse had chewed through a
picture of Uncle Bramble. There was a hole right in the
middle of his face. But Rosie wasn't mad. She had
never been fond of Uncle Bramble, anyway.

After Rosie dressed for bed that night, she put on her favorite slippers. But one toe stuck out of the end of her slipper. The mouse had chewed a hole in it!

Rosie threw the slippers away.

"This is too much," Rosie said to herself.

"Those were my favorite slippers."

Rosie calmed herself down and curled up with a good book in front of the fire. But the mouse had found the book, too. When she opened it, there were so many holes in the pages, she couldn't read it at all!

Rosie slammed the book down on the table. "This is the last straw!" she said. "I have to get rid of that mouse!"

Rosie didn't move. She just sat and thought.

Finally Rosie had an idea. She called her sister
and asked if she could borrow her cat, Fred, for a while.
"Of course, you may," her sister said.

After the phone call, Rosie felt much better.
Fred would be a help. "No mouse would want to live
in a house with a cat like Fred," Rosie said out loud,
hoping the mouse would hear her.

In the morning Rosie went to get Fred. Fred was an
enormous orange cat that just loved to catch mice.
Rosie's sister said she hadn't had a single mouse in her
house since she got Fred.

When they got back home, Fred sniffed here and there. He knew there was a mouse in the house. After he sniffed, Fred sat in the middle of the living room, waiting for the mouse to appear. But the mouse didn't show up.

Later, while Rosie was relaxing in front of the TV, she heard terrible squeaking and growling noises in the kitchen.

"Gracious!" said Rosie. "What is all that ruckus?"

Rosie rushed to the kitchen. There in the corner, frightened out of his wits, was the little brown mouse. He was squeaking at the top of his lungs. Fred was growling at him, ready to attack.

Just before Fred pounced, Rosie grabbed the mouse and stuck him in an empty coffee can. Then she poked holes in the plastic lid so the little mouse could breathe.

Rosie was very upset. Fred had nearly killed the mouse. Rosie wanted to get rid of the mouse, but she didn't want him hurt. She had hoped that he would see Fred the cat and just leave.

"Poor little mouse!" she thought. "He looked so scared."

Rosie packed up Fred and the coffee can with
the mouse in it and drove to her sister's house.

After dropping Fred off at her sister's, Rosie drove and drove. Finally she stopped beside a field miles from her home. She took the mouse out of the coffee can and patted his little head.

"You're a nice mouse," she said. "But you're too messy." She sat him down on the ground. "Good-bye, Mr. Mouse."

ROSIE

The little mouse just sat there at the side of the road and looked up at Rosie. Rosie got into her car and drove home.

Days passed. Rosie slept well at night. She did not find holes chewed in her shoes. She didn't have a mouse in her sugar bowl. There was no mouse under the bedcovers. Her neat little life was back to normal. And that was how Rosie liked it.

Except sometimes. Sometimes she would get lonely, especially at night when her house seemed just too quiet and too neat. Sometimes she even missed the little mouse.

One night, when Rosie was especially tired and cold, she fell asleep in front of the fireplace. When she woke up, it was very late. She stumbled to the bathroom to brush her teeth, then climbed into bed and went back to sleep.

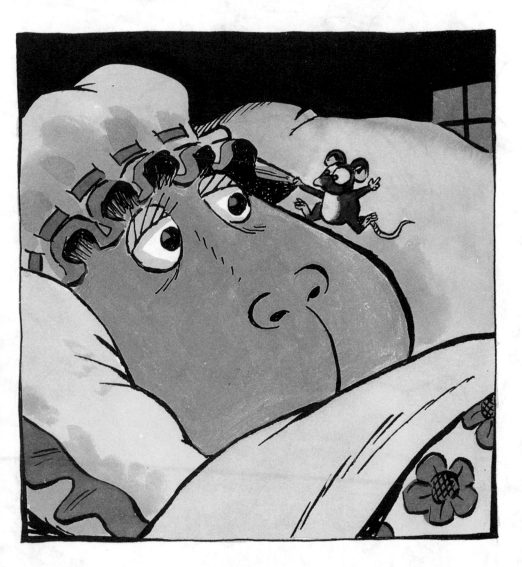

She had been asleep for quite a while when she was
awakened by a squeaking noise. She listened. It grew
louder. Then Rosie felt a little tug at her nightcap.

Rosie quickly turned on the light. There, sitting on her pillow, was the little brown mouse. He was back, but this time he didn't run away. He jumped up and down, trying to get her attention.

"Oh, drat!" said Rosie. "How did you ever find your way back here?"

Then Rosie smelled something. It was smoke. She stuck the little mouse in her pocket and went to the living room.

A hot coal had popped out of the fireplace and landed on the rug. The rug was smoking. Rosie quickly poured water on it and put out the fire. Because of the mouse, she had caught it just in time.

Rosie was shaking all over. She picked up the
little mouse. "You saved my life," she said.
And she hugged him.

Then she and the brown mouse went back into the bedroom. Rosie found a shoe box and a towel and made a little bed. She put the mouse in it and placed the box next to her pillow. They slept together all night long.

News about Rosie and her mouse spread all around town. A reporter from the town newspaper did a story on them. They even had their picture taken. Rosie and her mouse grew famous.

Rosie still lives in the same pink house with the same little yard. But she doesn't live alone anymore. And her house isn't quite as neat anymore. But Rosie doesn't mind—because she never *ever* grows lonely at night.